Emily,

May all your dreams come true!

♡ J.J.

Casey & Bella

Casey and Bella

GO TO
HAWAII

Written by Jane Lovascio

Story Idea by Lacey Hickey

Illustrated by Aija Jasuna

Publishers Cataloging-in-Publication Data

Lovascio, Jane.
    Casey and Bella go to Hawaii / written by Jane Lovascio ;
illustrated by Aija Jasuna.
        p. cm.
    Summary: Two dogs spend a day surfing, hula dancing, and exploring
Hawaii. Along the way, they make a few new friends and encourage them
to follow their dreams.
    ISBN-13: 978-1-60131-077-4
    [1. Dogs—Juvenile fiction. 2. Hawaii—Juvenile fiction. 3. Friendship—
Juvenile fiction. 4. Happiness—Juvenile fiction. 5. Stories in rhyme.]
I. Jasuna, Aija, ill. II. Title.

                                        2010942072

Big Tent Books

115 Bluebill Drive
Savannah, GA 31419
United States
(888) 300-1961

To order additional copies please go to www.CaseyAndBella.com

This book was published with the assistance of the helpful folks at DragonPencil.com

CPSIA facility code: BP 305988

Dedicated to all the Casey and Bella
authors out there!

"In order to live the life of your dreams,
you must first dream of the life you want
to live."
                              —Jane Lovascio

Casey and Bella support Jumpstart, www.jstart.org

Jumpstart is dedicated to helping preschool children succeed
in school and in life. Learn more at www.jstart.org.

Casey and Bella woke up to find Jane
packing up her suitcase.
"We're going on a trip!"
Jane announced with a smile on her face.

"Let's go," called Jeff. "We don't want to miss the plane."
"I wonder where we are going," thought Bella,
as they followed alongside Jane.

Eleven hours later, they arrived at the airport in Honolulu. Casey and Bella wagged their tails as they thought about all they would do.

"Aloha, and welcome to Hawaii," said the hula dancers. "We hope you enjoy your stay." Jane and Jeff were given flower leis, as Casey and Bella ran off to play.

The hotel in Oahu looked like a postcard with
a view of the turquoise ocean.
Casey and Bella took a peek at the itinerary,
while Jane and Jeff put on their suntan lotion.

"Surfing, hula dancing, wow," barked Bella,
"even a tour of volcanoes!"
"There is so much to do, but so little
time," sighed Casey. "We'll have to
see how the day goes."

After a delicious lunch, Jane and Jeff departed for their island tour.
"Come on, Casey," begged Bella, "now is our chance. We must go out and explore!"

"Let's go surfing," declared Casey.
"But I want to hula dance," Bella said.
When they arrived at Waikiki beach, they decided to split up instead.

Bella stayed on the beach, while Casey dashed toward the sea.
"We'll meet up when we're done," said Casey. "Let's meet at a quarter 'til three."
Casey looked at the crashing waves and started to feel all flustered.
"Don't be scared," said a crab. "I'll help you. I'm Gina, the surf instructor."

"Surf's up!" Gina shouted. "Grab your boards and follow me into the water."
Casey was nervous, because she had already forgotten everything Gina had taught her.

"Remember to pop up on your board," said Gina, "and don't worry if you wipeout."
Casey noticed Gina looked sad as she escorted the surfers out.

"Gina," said Casey, "can I ask you
a couple of questions?
Are you happy with your job?
Do you like giving surfing lessons?"

"Actually," Gina replied, "my dream is to design
surfboards and then sell them at my own store.
Then I could watch all the surfers ride my boards
on the waves of the North Shore."

"Sounds like a wonderful dream," said Casey with compassion.
"If you follow your dreams, you will always be happy.
You will live with purpose and passion."

"Thanks for the advice," Gina said in a happy tone.
Then Gina swam away, and Casey was all alone.

As Casey floated on her board,
her fur began to quiver.
She was too scared to surf the big waves,
and the cold water made her shiver.

Then, as Casey was ready to give up,
A dolphin appeared and said, "What's wrong, little pup?"

"I am afraid," said Casey. "I am not ready to surf the waves today.
Maybe I should go check on Bella. I think I'll call it a day."

"My name is Kai," said the dolphin. "Let me give you a friendly tip.
If you believe in yourself, you can do anything!"
he squeaked as he was doing a flip.

Before Casey could thank Kai,
he disappeared quickly into the ocean.
Then Casey felt a burst of courage
and was filled up with emotion.

Casey began to believe in herself
just as a humongous wave appeared.
"Cowabunga! Banzai!" Casey yelled.
It was exactly what she had feared.

Her heart was pumping, dolphins were jumping,
as her spirit began to soar.
Bella scurried to greet Casey on the beach,
as she rode the big wave to shore.

"You did it! Great job!" Bella cheered loudly as Casey proudly returned.
"Now come meet Tina, my hula instructor, and I'll show you what I have learned!"

When Bella introduced her hula instructor, Casey looked puzzled and scratched her head.
"You look exactly like my surf instructor, but her name was Gina," Casey said.

"That is because we are twins," said Tina. "Can't you tell us apart by our claws?"
"Yours are blue, and Gina's are red!" Casey proclaimed as she happily licked her paws.

Bella began to hula, while Tina yelled out helpful tips.
"Start with lewa or the leg lift; then 'ami, roll your hips!"

"Next can we go to the Big Island?" begged Bella. "Can we go on a volcano tour?"
"Would you like to come with us, Tina?" asked Casey. "Please come join us as we explore."

"Thanks for asking. I'd love to go!" Tina quickly replied.
"I will call my friend, Keanu, and ask if he'll give us a ride."

As they patiently waited for Keanu, they all
sipped on some pineapple juice.
Finally he arrived. "Aloha," he honked,
"I am Keanu, the Hawaiian goose."

Casey, Bella, and Tina followed him to
his boss' chopper.
"He runs a tour every day from Oahu,"
said Keanu. "I'll sneak us onto his helicopter!"

They hid under the cargo net, as the helicopter began to take flight.
The rainforest, waterfalls, and volcanoes were such a beautiful sight.

They saw the steam from the vents of Kilauea
and felt the heat from the lava below.
Bella barked with excitement at the black sand beaches
created by the volcano.

When the helicopter landed on the Big Island,
they were all eager to explore.
"Hi, I am Danny," said a dachshund.
"You're just in time for the tour!"

"Excuse me, Danny, are you hiring?" inquired Tina.
"Because I would love to join your team.
I would love to work at a volcano;
it has always been my dream!"

"Why, yes!" barked Danny. "Today is your lucky day! I am ready to retire. Can you start right away?"

Tina happily accepted, so Casey and Bella had to say goodbye. They snuck back onto the chopper and waved to Tina as it began to fly.

They landed back in Oahu. It was finally the end of the tour.
"How will we ever get back to Waikiki," asked Casey,
"when we landed at the North Shore?"
Casey started to get nervous. "Come on, Bella, it's late.
It's time for us to head back!"
Then, all of a sudden, they saw their friend Gina
painting a sign on her new surf shack.

"I followed my dreams," said Gina, "and now I am happier than ever! As a thank you, please take one of my surfboards, so you will remember this trip forever."

"Wow, thanks!" said Casey. "I will think of Hawaii whenever I surf the sea. It's getting really late though; can you help us get back to Waikiki?"

DOLPHIN EXPRESS

"We'll whistle for the Dolphin Express," said Gina. "Follow me down to the bay.
Don't worry, you'll be home in time; this is the fastest way!"

Casey was happy to see it was Kai who popped out from the water,
Because she finally got to thank him for the wonderful lesson he taught her.

When they got back to the hotel, Casey and Bella quickly scurried up to their room. "Hurry up," shouted Casey. "Shake off the sand and change your clothes. Jeff and Jane will be home soon!"

"We're back," said Jeff. "We took pictures of the places we explored."
"Wait a minute," said Jane.
"Do you remember buying this surfboard?"

Casey and Bella go to Hawaii
By Lacey Hickey

One early morning, Casey woke up and saw Jane and Jeff packing. "Bella, Bella" Casey yelled "I think we are going on vacation!"

"Really?" Bella asked.

"Positive!" Casey remarked.

Jane walked in the room and grabbed Casey and Bella. "Come, come." She told them. "We don't want to miss the plane. Daddy has your toys and treats girls; let's get in the car."

Bella yelps, "I'm excited; I wonder where we are going Casey?"

"I don't know, but I'm sure it will be fun." Jane had planned for the family to go to Hawaii. When she told the dogs they couldn't wait!

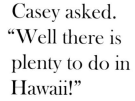

"We're here! We're here, we are really here!" Bella shouted.

"I wonder what we could do." Casey asked. "Well there is plenty to do in Hawaii!"

Jane and Jeff took Casey and Bella up to their hotel room, and Casey was thinking about what they could do. "Let's see what you have planned for us Casey:

1. Windsurfing,
2. Hula dancing,
3. A tour of the volcanoes,
4. And Surfing."

"This sounds like a fun-packed vacation you planned for us, thanks Casey." Bella said.

When Jane and Jeff went to get lunch, that is when Casey and Bella made their move to see Hawaii and do all the activities on their list.

"Ok first thing is windsurfing." Casey said. "Hello, my name is Gina the Crab, and I will be teaching you how to windsurf." Said Gina.

"Oh, well hi there, we are Casey and Bella." Bella told Gina.

"Well let's get you out in the ocean. First, just step on the board and point the sail what direction you want to go in. Ok, ready, GO!"

"That was so fun!" Casey yelled.

"Um, Gina, I have a question for you." Bella told her.

"Ask away," Gina said .

"Well do you actually like your job?" she asked.

"No, I don't want to do this, I wanted to own my very own surf shop, but my mom made me do this!" She whined.

"Well if you don't like doing this you shouldn't. Do what you want to do, not what someone tells you." Bella told her.

"I agree with Bella, Gina. Just follow your dream." Casey told Gina.

"Well ok, thanks." Gina remarked.

"We have to go now." Bella told Casey.

"Bye Gina!", they both yelled as they walked away.

"Hello I am Tina, and I am your hula dance instructor."

"Why, hello," the girls answered. Casey and Bella were thinking this person would be very happy, because she gets to dance all day. But no, Tina wasn't like that. In fact Tina told the girls she never wanted to do this!

"Well then, what do you want to do Tina?"

"I have always wanted to be a volcano rock collector." She told Casey.

"Well we want you to do what you want to do. Don't dance if you don't want to." Bella explained.

"Thank you," said Tina as she ran off to tour the Hawaiian volcanoes."

"Welcome I am Danny the Daschund, and I would be pleased to take you on your tour today. As we pass the last volcano on our tour we would like to point out the rock collectors." Danny told the group.

"Look there is Tina. How do you like rock collecting Tina?" asked Casey.

"It is great; if it weren't for you and Bella I would have never have followed my dream. Thank you!" Shouted Tina.

"I think I am a little tired to go surfing." Casey cried.

"Well ok, but I want to stop and buy a surfboard, maybe during the summer Jane and Jeff would take us to the beach." Bella told Casey.

As Casey and Bella arrived at the surf shack they saw Gina. "Gina you decided to run the surfboard shack!" Bella yelped with joy.

"Yeah, and I am so happy." Said Gina.

"I am glad you followed your dream Gina." Casey told her.

"We really need to get back to the hotel though. Please give us one pink surfboard." Casey asked. "Bella we have to make it back quick, let's go!" Casey shouted.

"It is time to pack girls, hey where did this little pink surfboard come from?" Jane asked.

Casey and Bella were caught. "I guess we could bring the surfboard back home, we would just have to go to the beach." Jane exclaimed.

On the plane ride home there were Casey and Bella sleeping, dreaming of what their next adventure would be.

Lacey is very proud to be the co-author for *Casey and Bella Go to Hawaii*. She wants to be a famous author when she gets older, and this opportunity is helping her reach that goal. Lacey is a fifth-grader at Millstone Township Elementary School; and if she didn't attend this school, she would have never had this incredible opportunity.

Lacey plays competitive travel softball and must divide her time between her two favorite passions. So, when she does write, her stories are very well-planned.

Lacey would like to thank her family for all their support in everything she does. This has been a chance of a lifetime. She LOVES writing, and her dreams are coming true!

Lacey Hickey

Enter the Casey and Bella™ Writing Contest and become a published author!

Third, fourth, and fifth graders who are residents of the United States or Canada are eligible to enter.

The Grand Prize Winner: receives a $500.00 cash prize, plaque, certificate, and his/her story idea will be developed and written by the author, then professionally illustrated and published by Big Tent Books the following year as the next book in the Casey and Bella™ book series!

The grand prize winner will be credited for his/her story idea on the dedication page inside the book. The winner's story will also be published inside the book. The author will travel to the winner's school to present the award and read the finished story. Winner will also receive a personalized signed book and photo with the author.

First Place: Winner will receive an engraved plaque with the child's name and certificate to honor his/her work. The author will travel to the winner's school to present the award. Winner will also receive a personalized signed book and photo with the author.

Second and Third Place: Winner will receive a certificate to honor his/her work. The author will travel to the winner's school to present the award. Winner will also receive a personalized signed book and photo with the author.

Visit www.CaseyAndBella.com for full details.

www.CaseyAndBella.com

CUDDL BOOKS INC

FREE GAMES!
SAFE FUN
FOR ALL AGES.